The Mushas Make a Stink

WE NEED TO TURN THE MAGIC ON.
WE NEED TO SAVE THE DAY.
COME ON!

"Hello! It's time for some more fun in Treetopolis, but first we need to do the moves that turn our magic powers on. Come on, join in!

TIME FOR TREE FU!

To make Tree Fu spells do what you see . . .
Slide to the side, and **jump** right back!
Hold your hands up high, **spin** around . . .
Reach up for the sky!

Look, the sapstone in my belt is **glowing**! Moving turned our magic on. Thanks for your help!"

Tom arrived in Treetopolis to find Twigs decorating Ariela's barn. "What are you up to?" he asked.
"Today is Sap Day, Tom!" said Twigs excitedly.
"It's the one day of the year when the sap fountain erupts and we celebrate and give thanks for magic,"
Ariela explained.

"And we eat Sap Day buns!" Twigs added.
"In fact, I want a bun right now. Let's
hurry and get this decorating done!"
So Twigs quickly did a *Magic Twin* spell,
which made him appear twice.

MAGIC TWIN!

"Two Twigs? Double trouble!" laughed Tom.
Both Twigs flew around the barn at top speed, decorating as
they went. But they quickly got tangled up in the bunting and
fell to the floor!
"*Two back to one.* Well, that didn't quite go as planned!"
Twigs said, as the other Twigs disappeared.

Meanwhile, the Mushas, Stink and Puffy, were not very happy. "I don't like Sap Day. It's not fair that Sprites can do magic and Mushas can't," huffed Puffy.
"Yeah! Rubbish Sap Day celebration," Stink agreed.

Feeling annoyed, Stink kicked a round mushroom, which puffed out a very smelly yellow cloud.
"That's horrible! I *love* it!" Puffy cried.
"Ooh! Let's use these to turn Sap Day into Stink Day!" Stink laughed, grabbing lots of round mushrooms.

Twigs had finally finished putting up the decorations and was just about to take a bite of his first Sap Day bun, when he spotted some strange yellow clouds in the sky.
"What are those?" he wondered. But no one knew.
"Let's find out!" suggested Tom.

Stink and Puffy also spotted something. It was Squirmtum. "Happy Stink Day!" they called, as they squashed a round mushroom.

The smelly yellow cloud blew over Squirmtum and he suddenly fell fast asleep. Stink and Puffy thought it was brilliant! Stink Day would be even more fun now!

The Mushas set off to cause more mischief, and they didn't notice when Flicker flew out of Squirmtum's helmet to find help.

As Tom, Twigs and Ariela were flying towards the yellow clouds, they met Flicker. "Hey, little fella! What's the matter?" Ariela asked.
Flicker buzzed at them. "I think he wants us to follow him," said Tom.

ZZZZZZ

"Squirmtum's asleep,"
Ariela said, when Flicker led
them to him. "And he stinks!"
Twigs shouted loudly but couldn't wake
him. "Wowzers, someone must've
put a spell on him!" he cried.
"It must be a very strong spell,"
Tom said, after he'd tried the
Rise and Shine spell and
Squirmtum kept on snoring.

Next, Stink and Puffy used the yellow clouds to make Rickety fall asleep. They also used them to change his Sap Day buns into Stink Day buns, laughing as they quickly scoffed them all.

ZZZZZZ

Tom, Twigs and Ariela found Rickety sound asleep under a yellow cloud, just like Squirmtum! "What's going on?" Twigs wondered. "I don't know, but I've got a feeling those yellow clouds have something to do with it," Tom replied.

They followed the yellow clouds to the castle, where they saw Puffy and Stink driving around in Zigzoo's wagon, squashing mushrooms and putting everyone to sleep.
"It's the Mushas!" Tom gasped.
"We've got to stop them!"

Tom, Twigs and Ariela chased after Stink and Puffy as fast as they could. "I'll stop them! Yee ha!" Ariela cried, throwing her lasso. But she caught a mushroom, and as the rope tightened, a yellow cloud blew over her. Then she fell asleep, too!

"Oh no, not Ariela as well!" Tom cried, turning to Twigs. "No, wait!" he called, seeing that Twigs was reaching for a green bun. "That's not a Sap Day bun, it's a Stink Day bun!" But his warning was too late. Twigs had already taken a bite and fallen fast asleep.

"What am I going to do now?" Tom wondered. "How can I stop the Mushas without my friends' help?"

"I know, I'll ask Treetog," Tom decided.
But when he arrived in the Tower Library,
he found Treetog fast asleep, too!
Then Tom noticed that a page was open in
Treetog's spell book. It said that the smell of
the blue Sap Flowers could wake everyone up
from the sleep caused by the yellow clouds.
Now Tom knew what he had to do!

Back down in the city streets, Tom saw that there were enough flowers to wake everyone. But the Mushas were there, too. "Without my friends to help me, how can I get to the flowers?" he thought. "Aha! I know what Twigs would do!"

"Hey! You can't get me!"
called Tom, teasing the Mushas.
"Yes we can. Happy Stink Day!" shouted Puffy, squashing their very
last mushroom at him. But it wasn't Tom, it was Tom Two! He'd
used Twigs' *Magic Twin* spell! This second Tom then disappeared.
With no mushrooms left, the Mushas ran away in fright!

"Now there's only one of me again, we need to use **BIG WORLD MAGIC** to spread the smell of the Sap Flowers around Treetopolis to wake everyone up. It's time to do the *Blow-Blow-Blow* spell. Are you ready?"

TREE FU GO!

"Copy me, into your spell pose."

"Spin your hands around each other, then stop."

"Hold one hand out, then touch your shoulder and push out."

"Hold the other hand out, then touch your shoulder and push out."

"Swing both arms up, then swing down."

"Swing up again, then swing down, then up and jump."

"Now clap and say 'Blow-Blow-Blow' to send the magic to me. Blow-Blow-Blow!"

"Yes, we did it! Thanks for your help!"

A magic wind blew the smell of Sap Flowers all around Treetopolis, waking everyone up.

"Yuck, I hate the smell of flowers!" Puffy cried when the wind blew by.

"Me, too!" agreed Stink, as they rushed home.

WHOOOOSH!

As the sap fountain erupted, Tom told his friends that he'd used Twigs' spell.

"You see, when you have real friends, you're never truly alone," said Treetog.

"She's right! Happy Sap Day, bestest buddy!" Twigs said with his mouth full of Sap Day bun, as everyone laughed.

Thanks for helping me in Treetopolis, see you soon
for another adventure. Bye for now!

TREE
FU TOM: THE
MUSHAS MAKE A STINK
A BANTAM BOOK
978 0 857 51166 9

Published in Great Britain
by Bantam, an imprint of Random House
Children's Publishers UK
A Random House Group Company.

This edition published 2013

1 3 5 7 9 10 8 6 4 2

Tree Fu Tom created by Daniel Bays.
Based on the episode 'Sappy Day', written by Davey Moore and Douglas Wood.
TREE FU TOM word and device marks are trade marks of the British Broadcasting
Corporation and FremantleMedia Enterprises and are used under licence. TREE FU TOM
device marks © BBC and FremantleMedia Enterprises MMX. The "BBC" word mark and
logo are trade marks of the British Broadcasting Corporation and are used under licence.
BBC Logo © BBC 1996. Licensed by FremantleMedia Enterprises.

Bantam Books are published by Random House Children's Publishers UK,
61-63 Uxbridge Road, London W5 5SA

www.randomhousechildrens.co.uk

Addresses for companies within The Random House Group Limited can be found at:
www.randomhouse.co.uk/offices.htm

THE RANDOM HOUSE GROUP Limited Reg. No. 954009

A CIP catalogue record for this book is available
from the British Library

Printed in China

MIX
Paper from
responsible sources
FSC® C104723